SOFIA MARTINEZ

The Beach Trip

by Jacqueline Jules

illustrated by Kim Smith

PICTURE WINDOW BOOKS
a capstone imprint

Sofia Martinez is published by
Picture Window Books, a Capstone imprint
1710 Roe Crest Drive
North Mankato, MN 56003
www.mycapstone.com

Library of Congress Cataloging-in-Publication Data
is available on the Library of Congress web site.

ISBN: 978-1-4795-8719-3 (library binding)
ISBN: 978-1-4795-8725-4 (paperback)
ISBN: 978-1-4795-8729-2 (eBook pdf)

Summary: Sofia and her family are headed to the
beach for the weekend, and Sofia is packed and
ready to go. But once they get to the beach house, it's
obvious that Sofia did not pack basic beach gear. Will
her beach trip be ruined? Spanish words are used
throughout this early chapter book.

Designer: Kay Fraser

Printed in China.
009465F16

TABLE OF CONTENTS

CHAPTER 1

Packing Problems

The yearly beach trip was tomorrow. It took six hours to get to the beach house, but the trip was worth it. Sixteen family members in one house was so fun!

Sofia carried a pile of board games upstairs.

"You're supposed to be packing

for the beach," Mamá said.

"Yo sé," Sofia said. "I need these

for the trip."

Mamá frowned. "You need clothes

and a swimsuit. Not games."

"But the twins will be there! Camila and Valeria love games," Sofia said.

"That's when it is cold. You should be outside when it's warm," Mamá said.

"Por favor," Sofia begged.

"You can bring one game,"
Mamá said.

But it wasn't easy to choose.
Camila liked one game better.
Valeria liked another one. And
Sofia couldn't leave behind her
own favorite game.

"I'll need all three," she said.

Sofia put them into her suitcase. She had no room left for clothes.

"Can I put some shorts and shirts in your suitcase?" Sofia asked her big sister, Luisa.

"I have room for one outfit," Luisa said.

Her other sister, Elena, packed
Sofia's swimsuit. Now Sofia was
packed and ready to go!

Sofia would not have many
clothes for her trip. But she would
have plenty of games, and that is
what she really needed.

CHAPTER 2

Too Much Stuff

The next morning, Papá and Tío Miguel were packing the cars in the driveway. They packed suitcases, beach bags, and coolers. The trunks were stuffed!

"¡No más!" Papá said.

"But we haven't put in Mariela's stroller or our beach bags," Tía Carmen said.

"I think we need to drive three cars," Mamá said.

"¡Claro!" Tío Miguel agreed. "We can follow each other."

He went across the yard to get his car.

"I'll take baby Mariela and Manuel," Tía Carmen said. "Who else wants to go with me?"

Sofia shook her head. Manuel got car sick. Baby Mariela cried a lot.

"I'd love to," Mamá said.

That left Sofia's two oldest cousins, her two big sisters, Tío Miguel, Papá, and Abuela.

"The girls can ride with me," Papá said. "The boys can go with Tío Miguel and Abuela."

They were finally ready to go! Before long, Sofia was sorry she was riding with her sisters.

"Luisa is bothering me," Elena said.

"Elena is bothering me more!"
Luisa said.

They were so loud, Sofia couldn't
read her book.

At the first stop, Sofia hopped
into Tío Miguel's car.

"Do you have room for one more?" Sofia asked.

"¡Claro!" Tío Miguel said.

But the ride wasn't much better. Hector and Alonzo squirmed and kicked each other.

After lunch, Sofia asked to ride in the last car. Baby Mariela and Manuel fell asleep.

"Finally!" Sofia said, smiling. "Silencio."

CHAPTER 3

No Sun

They arrived at the beach house before dinner. The twins and their parents were already there.

"After that long drive, nobody is up for cooking. Let's go out for dinner," Abuela said.

The twins changed into sundresses. Sofia only had one change of clothes for the whole week, so she couldn't change.

"I brought an extra dress," Camila said. "You can borrow it."

"Gracias," Sofia said.

At dinner, the family talked about going to the beach the next day.

"I can't wait for the waves," Tío Miguel said.

"The sand is the best," Valeria said. "It's so soft."

"I want to make a giant sandcastle," Hector said.

When they went to bed, Sofia realized she was missing something else.

"Do you have extra pajamas?" she asked Valeria.

"I sure do," Camila said.

In the morning, everyone jumped out of bed, ready for the beach. But the sun was not shining.

Instead, it was raining. Sixteen people were stuck inside.

"This might be a long day," Tía Carmen said.

"There isn't even a TV here," Luisa said.

"We can still have fun," Sofia said. "Just wait."

She ran upstairs to get her suitcase and dragged it downstairs.

"¡Oh dios mío! You only packed games?" Mamá asked. "Where are your clothes?"

"I have one outfit and a swimsuit," Sofia said.

"My sweet Sofia," **Abuela** said. "You always make things interesting."

"It's okay. We can all share clothes," Camila said. "Right now we need something to play."

"**Sí**," Valeria agreed.

Kids and parents counted paper money. They rolled dice. They moved pieces around game boards.

Everyone was busy until just after lunch when **Abuela** looked out the window.

"¡**El sol!**" she said.

"¡Vámonos!" Tío Miguel shouted.

Ten minutes later, sixteen people were at the beach.

"This is the perfect beach day," Abuela said.

"It sure is," Sofia said. "Games, fun, and sun."

Spanish Glossary

abuela — grandmother

claro — of course

el sol — the sun

gracias — thank you

mamá — mom

no más — no more

oh dios mío — oh my goodness

papá — dad

por favor — please

sí — yes

silencio — silence

tía — aunt

tío — uncle

vámonos — let's go

yo sé — I know

Talk It Out

1. Sofia's mom told her to pack just one game, but Sofia didn't listen. Should Sofia get in trouble? Why or why not?

2. Were you able to predict that it was going to rain? Were there any clues in the story?

3. How do you think Sofia felt when she saved the day with her games?

Write It Down

1. Sofia and her family went to the beach for vacation. Write about your dream vacation.

2. The trip to the beach took six hours. Make a list of items you would bring in the car if you took a long road trip.

3. If you could only pack three items, what would you pack? Write a paragraph describing your answer.

About the Author

Jacqueline Jules is the award-winning author of thirty children's books, including *No English* (2012 Forward National Literature Award), *Zapato Power: Freddie Ramos Takes Off* (2010 Cybils Literary Award, Maryland Blue Crab Young Reader Honor Award, and ALSC Great Early Elementary Reads), and *Freddie Ramos Makes a Splash* (named on 2013 List of Best Children's Books of the Year by the Bank Street College Committee).

When not reading, writing, or teaching, Jacqueline enjoys time with her family in northern Virginia.

About the Illustrator

Kim Smith has worked in magazines, advertising, animation, and children's gaming. She studied illustration at the Alberta College of Art and Design in Calgary, Alberta.

Kim has illustrated several picture books, including *Home Alone: the Classic Illustrated Storybook* (Quirk Books), *Over the River and Through the Woods* (Sterling), and *A Ticket Around the World* (Owlkids Books). She lives in Calgary with her husband, Eric, and dog, Whisky.

FUN
doesn't stop here!

- Videos & Contests
- Games & Puzzles
- Friends & Favorites
- Authors & Illustrators

Discover more at
www.capstonekids.com

See you soon!
¡Nos vemos pronto!